Lee Henry's Best Friend

Judy Delton
Pictures by **John Faulkner**

Albert Whitman & Company, Chicago

Library of Congress Cataloging in Publication Data

Delton, Judy.
  Lee Henry's best friend.

  (A Concept book)
  SUMMARY: Lee Henry's best friend moves away, leaving
Lee Henry with a bad case of the blues and the conviction
that he'll never make another friend.
  [1. Moving, Household — Fiction. 2. Friendship —
Fiction] I. Faulkner, John Frink, 1922-   II. Title.
PZ7.D388Le   [E]   79-16902
ISBN 0-8075-4417-5

Text © 1980 by Judy Delton
Illustrations © 1980 by John Faulkner
Published simultaneously in Canada by
General Publishing, Limited, Toronto

*For Bev, Mary Jo, Sandy, Margi,
Laura, and all the Wednesday
workshop scribes, past and present.*

Blair Andrew is my best friend.
When we play baseball, he says,
"Lee Henry, you can be first up to bat."
He takes turns.

He never cheats at games, like some guys.
And when he sleeps overnight at my house,
he never takes all the blankets.
He shares.

Blair Andrew can climb higher than me
in our oak tree, and he isn't scared in
the haunted house at the fair.

SPIDER

At school when I gave my talk about spiders
and everyone said they already knew about them,
Blair Andrew clapped for me.
He was the only one.

And when Mr. Maxwell said I threw the eraser,
Blair Andrew said Chris Richards did it,
even though he knew the kids
would call him a tattle-tale.

That's the kind of best friend Blair Andrew is.

Blair Andrew said he likes me best
of all the kids at school,
and I said I like him best.
We made up a special handshake
and a secret code
and promised never to like anyone better.
Especially girls and teachers.

Then an awful thing happened.

Blair Andrew's dad got a job in Cincinnati,
and the whole family had to move.

Blair Andrew said he wouldn't go
because we are best friends for life.

His mother said she understood
but that he had to move anyway.

Blair Andrew told me he would
run away on a freight train
or maybe we could run away together.

But Blair Andrew's dad heard us talking
and said, "You have to go with us,
Blair Andrew, and that's that!"

Blair Andrew's dad said we could
still be friends and write letters and
send pictures and visit sometimes.

That didn't sound like being
best friends to me.

"Things will be fine,"
Blair Andrew's dad said.

But things weren't fine at all.

Every day after Blair Andrew left,
I sat in our oak tree and missed him.

I didn't feel like eating, even at
Hamburger Island.

One day I got a letter from him.
He said he missed me, too,
and he hated his new school
and no one there knew how to
play baseball
as well as I do.
He said he would never have
a best friend again,
except for me.

"There are lots of nice kids around,"
said my mom. "You'll make new friends
and feel better after a while."

"There are NOT any nice kids," I
said. "And I'll never feel better!"
I slammed my bedroom door.

Then Monday when I was walking home from school, this new kid came up to me. I never saw him before in my life.

"I just moved here from California," this kid said. "Want to see the fort I built?"

I shrugged my shoulders.
"I don't care," I said. I didn't.

But there wasn't much else to do.

I went over to
the new kid's house.
His fort was okay.
We sat in it a while.
Then we played ball.

Tuesday after school
there was that kid again,
waiting for me.

"Come on over," he said.
"What for?" I asked.
"We could play a game."
"Do you cheat?" I asked.
"Of course not," the kid said.

We went over to his house and
set up the game. I won,
and he didn't even get mad.

By the time I got home it was late.
My mom said she'd been looking
all over for me.

"I was at a new kid's house," I said.

"Really? I'm glad you found a new
friend," said my mom.

"He's not my FRIEND," I said.
"Blair Andrew is my friend.
My very best friend."

"You can have more than one friend,
you know," said my mom.

Yesterday, there was that kid again.
"You could come over to my house,"
I said. "Do you like to climb trees?"

"Sure," he said.

When we were halfway up the oak tree,
I said, "You know, we can't be best
friends or anything. I already have
a best friend."

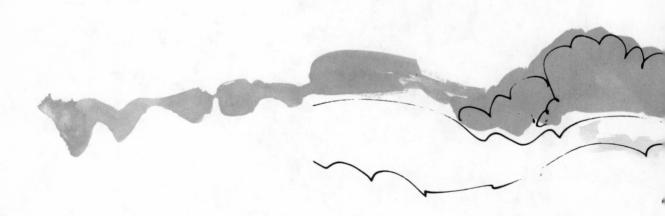

"That's okay," he said.
"I already have a best friend, too."

"You do?" I asked.

The kid nodded.
"He lives in California.
I had to move away, but
he's still my best friend."

"Of course," I said.

Tomorrow this new kid and I
are going to the museum.
He likes dinosaurs.
So do I.

I'll send Blair Andrew a postcard.
He's still my very best friend.

But this new kid is okay, too.

115306

DATE DUE

OCT 29 1983 NOV 1 6 2000		
NOV 1 9 1983		
DEC 1 0 1983	NOV 28 2002	
FEB 6 '84 DEC 1 7 84		
FEB 17 '84		
MAR 12 '84		
MAY 1 '84		
JUL 6 '84		
OCT 15 '86		
NOV 14 '86		
NOV 0 2 1988		
OCT 3 1 1989		

J
D
Delton, Judy
  Lee Henry's best friend.